This book is for O.

The art in this book was made with acrylic on paper.
The text was set in 26-point Zapatista.

Library of Congress Cataloging-in-Publication Data

Raschka, Christopher, author, illustrator.
Whaley Whale / Chris Raschka.
pages cm — (Thingy things)
Revised edition. Originally published by Hyperion Books for Children, 2000.
Summary: The reader is invited to find Whaley Whale's hiding place.
ISBN 978-1-4197-1058-2
[1. Whales—Fiction. 2. Hide-and-seek—Fiction.] I. Title.
PZ7.R1814Wh 2014
[E]—dc23
2013010331

Text and illustrations copyright © 2014 Chris Raschka
Book design by Meagan Bennett

Printed and bound in China
10 9 8 7 6 5 4 3 2 1

For bulk discount inquiries, contact specialsales@abramsbooks.com.

ABRAMS
THE ART OF BOOKS SINCE 1949
115 West 18th Street
New York, NY 10011
www.abramsbooks.com

CHRIS RASCHKA

WHALEY WHALE

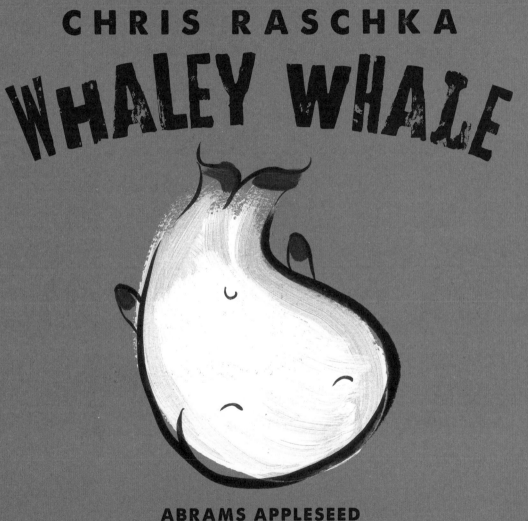

ABRAMS APPLESEED
NEW YORK

Whaley Whale is hiding.

Where is Whaley Whale?

Is she on the table?

No, Whaley Whale
is not on the table.

Is she in the basket?

Is she behind the door?

Is she under the chair?

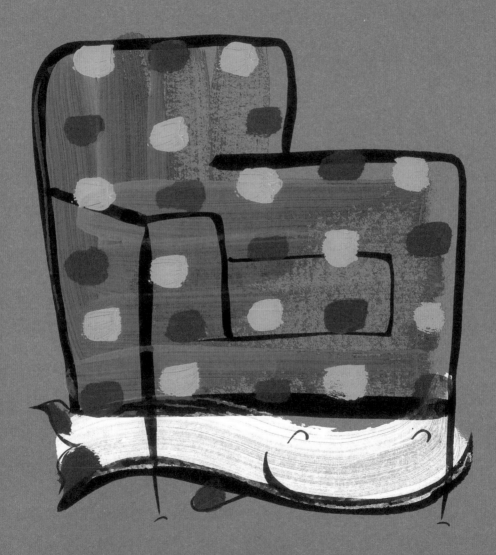

Whaley Whale!